More **Dark Man** books:

First series

Second series

Dark Man

Destiny in the Dark
by Peter Lancett
illustrated by Jan Pedroietta

Published by Ransom Publishing Ltd.
51 Southgate Street, Winchester, Hampshire SO23 9EH
www.ransom.co.uk

ISBN 978 184167 422 3

First published in 2005
Second printing 2007

A CIP catalogue record of this book is available from the British Library.

Dark Man

Destiny in the Dark

by Peter Lancett

illustrated by Jan Pedroietta

Ransom

Chapter One:
Night

The Old Man walks with the Dark Man.

They are in the bad part of the city.

It is night.

The streets are empty.

"This is the time when the Shadow Masters are strong," the Old Man says.

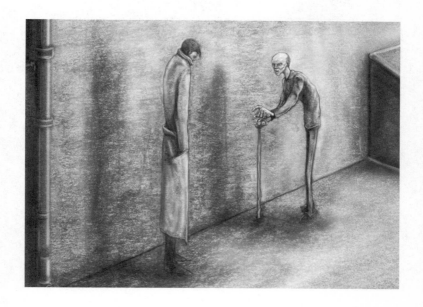

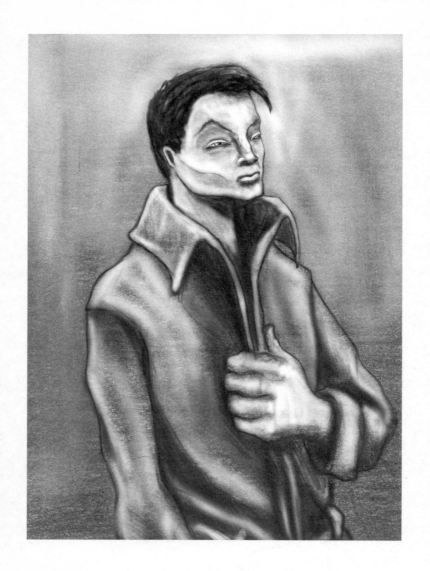

The Dark Man looks sad.

"I do what I can to stop them," he says.

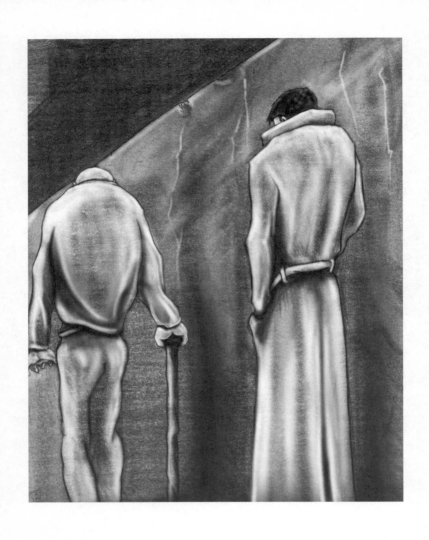

They keep walking, slowly.

Chapter Two:
The Golden Cup

The Old Man stops walking. He turns to the Dark Man.

"The Shadow Masters must never find the Golden Cup," he says.

The Dark Man is silent.

Then he says, "I do my best. I am only one man."

The Old Man nods.

"But you can work in the dark.

We cannot."

The Dark Man knows this.

The Old Man and the others like him are only strong in the light.

Chapter Three:
The Shadows

They walk some more.

The Dark Man looks into the shadows.

There is danger in this part of the city at night.

"We send help when we can," the Old Man says.

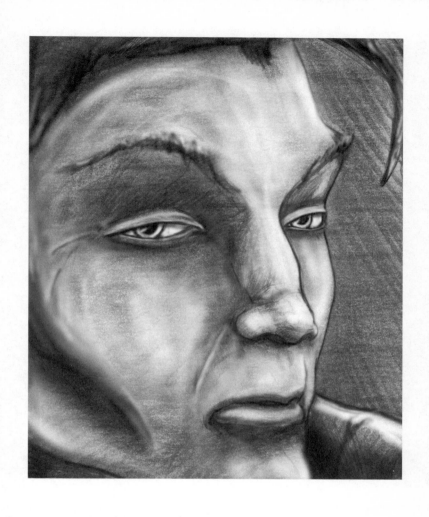

The Dark Man nods.

"When will this end?" he asks.

"When the Golden Cup is safe," the Old Man tells him.

Chapter Four:
Destiny

The Dark Man wants to ask many things.

He turns to the Old Man.

The Old Man is gone.

The Dark Man starts to walk.

He will keep helping the Old Man.

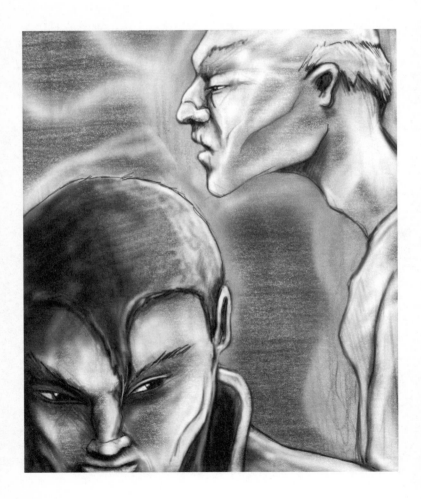

He must.

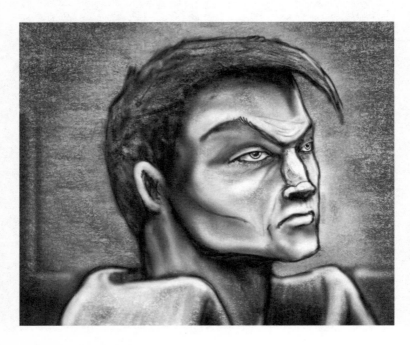

It is his destiny.

The author

photograph: Rachel Ottewill

Peter Lancett used to work in the
movies. Then he worked in the city.
Now he writes horror stories for a living.
"It beats having a proper job," he says.